*For Professor Martin Salisbury and the
amazing tutors at Cambridge School of Art*

MARGARET K. McELDERRY BOOKS
An imprint of Simon & Schuster Children's Publishing Division
1230 Avenue of the Americas, New York, New York 10020
Copyright © 2019 by Margarita Surnaite
Originally published in Great Britain by Anderson Press Ltd., London.

MARGARET K. McELDERRY BOOKS *is a trademark of Simon & Schuster, Inc.*
For information about special discounts for bulk purchases, please contact Simon & Schuster Special Sales
at 1-866-506-1949 or business@simonandschuster.com.
The Simon & Schuster Speakers Bureau can bring authors to your live event.
For more information or to book an event, contact the Simon & Schuster Speakers Bureau at 1-866-248-3049
or visit our website at www.simonspeakers.com.
The text for this book was set in Josefin Sans.
Manufactured in China
1218 SCP
First Margaret K. McElderry Books edition February 2019
2 4 6 8 10 9 7 5 3 1
Library of Congress Cataloging-in-Publication Data
Names: Surnaite, Margarita, author, illustrator.
Title: The lost book / Margarita Surnaite.
Description: First edition. | New York : Margaret K. McElderry Books, [2019] | Summary: "All rabbits love books,
except for Henry—he prefers games and adventures. But then he finds one very special book,
and when he reads it, someone very special finds him"— Provided by publisher.
Identifiers: LCCN 2018025692 (print) | LCCN 2018031574 (eBook)
ISBN 9781534438187 (hardback) | ISBN 9781534438194 (eBook)
Subjects: | CYAC: Books and reading--Fiction. | Lost and found possessions—Fiction. | Adventure and
adventurers—Fiction. | Rabbits—Fiction. | BISAC: JUVENILE FICTION / Animals / Rabbits. | JUVENILE
FICTION / Books & Libraries. | JUVENILE FICTION / Social Issues / Friendship.
Classification: LCC PZ7.1.S874 (eBook) | LCC PZ7.1.S874 Los 2019 (print) | DDC [E]—dc23
LC record available at https://lccn.loc.gov/2018025692

THE LOST BOOK

Margarita Surnaite

MARGARET K. McELDERRY BOOKS

New York   London   Toronto   Sydney   New Delhi

Henry lived in Rabbit Town with
his mom and dad, big sister Kate,
and little sister Amy.

In Rabbit Town, books were EVERYWHERE.
Rabbit adventures, rabbit history, rabbit food.

And all rabbits loved books . . .
except for Henry.

"What's so special about all these books?" he wondered.

"Games and real adventures are much more fun."

But then Henry found
the Lost Book.

It was not
a rabbit book.

"How did it get here?"
thought Henry.

"Did someone lose it?
Are they looking for it?"
But most of all, Henry
was curious to know . . .

. . . where it
had come
from.

He set off to find the owner
of the Lost Book.

But the creatures he met did not seem to care.

And they did not notice Henry,
who was beginning to feel
a little bit lost himself.

Just as he was about to lose hope,

Henry started to read the Lost Book and something amazing happened . . .

. . . almost.

"Excuse me," said the little creature. "I think you lost this."

It turned out there was one nice thing about getting lost:

being found.

Henry spent the afternoon with his new friend.

She showed him around the city.

And he found out about all of her favorite things.

He enjoyed himself so much, he forgot all about the Lost Book.

"Oh, my mom is here. I have to go," said the little creature.

Henry had a gift for his new friend, so she wouldn't forget him.

She had been so good at finding Henry and taking care of him, he knew the Lost Book would be in good hands.

"Mom, Dad, look—
it's a book!"

"You won't believe who I met today. He's sitting right . . ."

"Where did he go?"

"Henry! Where have you been?" asked his dad.

Henry just hugged everybody tightly.

That night, for the first time,
it was Henry who told the bedtime story.

An adventure so exciting,
it could have been in a book.